Encounters

2

A Bisexual Woman's

Introduction to FemDom

FFFM

Autumn Greer

Be sure to follow Autumn Greer on Amazon for notifications of new titles!

Enjoy and be sure to keep reading at the end for a Sneak Peek at Sleeping with the Enemy!

Romanceauthorcentral@gmail.com

CONTENTS

A Business Card

It was Monday, and Jan had woken up early.

As she prepared her usual breakfast (two scrambled eggs, with salt, freshly ground black pepper and sautéed bell peppers) she couldn't help but glance at the card each time she passed it. It hadn't moved from the place where she had set it the night before last after getting home from ***Encounters*** on Saturday. It was magnetizing. An unassuming black rectangular card, that held more promise than a piece of paper should be able to.

Before she realized what she was doing, she had brought her breakfast and cup of coffee to the table, where she normally never ate, to stare at the card.

She found herself unable to pull her eyes from the glossy black card, as if it might tell her what to do. She hadn't had her original dream again, now she dreamt only of Brie. The stunning woman who had dominated her, then taken Jan for herself at the club.

As they were leaving Encounters, Brie had given her the card.

The calling card was simple. An unassuming glossy black rectangle, the only writing on it was a phone number, in crisply contrasting white embossed letters.

What would be different if I called her? Jan thought to herself as she picked at her eggs, *Does she want me to go back to the club? Does she want to date?*

She toyed with the thought. Could she date a woman? She had never really considered it before. Did she want to date Brie or was she simply enamored with the way Brie had made her feel? She probably didn't even know her *real* name. What if Brie knows someone she knew? What if Brie was crazy?

Jan shook her head, maybe *she* was crazy. Sure, she had a fantastic time. She would remember that night at ***Encounters*** forever. *But…*

But, it was so taboo, what they had done, so unacceptable in daily life and modern culture. She couldn't pursue the Amazonian woman. She couldn't take a chance that someone in her personal or professional life might find out what Brie did, or what they had done together.

People might expect men to sleep around. And while women sleeping around and remaining unmarried *was* becoming more commonplace, it still wasn't socially acceptable or spoken of. And what they had done? That wasn't simply sleeping around.

No, she had to just enjoy the memories. The fantasy and remembering of the events of Saturday night would be enough. It had to be.

She couldn't eat with the butterflies in her stomach, still unsure of what to do (even though she knew what she *should* do). With a sigh, she stood and scraped her eggs into the waste basket, then took her dishes to the sink and looked at the clock on the stove. She set it a minute fast than the actual time so that she wouldn't be late getting out the door for work.

The illuminated green numbers of the clock told her it hadn't worked. She was late for work. The dishes would have to wait.

`*`

The workday was a drag. She slogged through her usual routine totally distracted. And before she knew it, it was Tuesday morning.

She made herself a bagel. Perhaps it was cooking her breakfast the day before that had made her lose track of the time.

She sat at her table, and that crisp black rectangle smiled back at her. In the two years she had lived in this house, she could count the number of times she had eaten at her kitchen table on one hand. Her normal breakfast spot was standing at her counter and shoveling her food down as quickly as possible. Not very ladylike, but that was what she was used to.

She set her phone on the table, face down and tried not to look at the card. But after a bite or two, and a sip of coffee, she was drawn back to the white numbers. Ten digits. She couldn't remember her own mother's cell number, but she knew the one from the black card of Brie's by heart already.

Maybe she would call it, and just see why Brie had given it to her. Perhaps it was like a review or feedback line, she scoffed at herself.

Yes, I was completely satisfied. Brie serviced me perfectly.

She reached forward, grabbed the card between her thumb and middle finger, and ran the tip of her index finger over the numbers.

The alarm on her cellphone went off. She jumped. Dammit. She had hardly touched her breakfast. She slapped the two halves of the bagel together, cream cheese to cream cheese, and poured the rest of her coffee into a travel mug. She wouldn't be late two days in a row. She was never late.

The Call

Thursday, Jan forced herself to eat at her breakfast bar. She didn't allow herself to sit at the table. She knew she couldn't entertain this fantasy any longer or she would give into a very stupid, impulsive desire. If she was being honest with herself, she wasn't even sure if it was simple curiosity or if she *really* just wanted to see Brie again.

Of course, everyone fantasized. Sometimes, she was sure women her age fantasized more than the men, if others were like her. The problem was that now she was fantasizing about something that only one person could give her. Or, at the very least, a fantasy that only one person she knew could satisfy.

She took a bite of her bagel and chewed it a little longer than she needed to and looked over her shoulder at the card. She couldn't. She walked across the room and grabbed the card. She tossed it into her junk drawer in the far-right kitchen cabinet and slammed it shut with a little more force than necessary.

She was a little early to leave for work. But to hell with it. Anything to distract her from that damn card.

`*`

Work didn't help.

She came home angry. After her first glass of wine, she had settled down some. When she went to pour a second glass, she grabbed the card from the drawer and brought it back with her to her armchair.

What was the worst that could come from one simple phone call? At least she would know why she was given the card. She wouldn't keep wondering. Then she could decide if she wanted to do…whatever it was Brie had in mind. She didn't *have* to do it. She didn't *have* to meet her again. But at least she would know and stop wondering.

Jan took a long pull from her glass, grabbed her phone, and entered the number into her cell from memory.

On the second ring, the voice answered the phone, "Yes?" So much promise in a single word.

Jan had to swallow before she could speak, "Maybe I shouldn't be calling." She said softly.

"I wondered if you would ever call. I recognize your voice. I know where we met. Don't worry. Your secrets are *always* safe with me. Its ok, I know why you're calling." The purr of the other woman's voice was enough to settle all of Jan's concerns and entice her all at once. She knew that wasn't an accident.

"I don't even know why I'm calling."

"I know why, and right now that's all you need to know. Its Friday night, you're probably not working tomorrow. This city is small enough to where I know you can be here in thirty minutes. Get a pen. Write down this address. Don't worry about what you're wearing I have everything you need here. And remember what I said. No one will ever know. See you in thirty minutes."

Behind the Gate

Jan hesitated when she saw the security guard at the entrance to the gated community. Surely, this security guard wouldn't let her through. What was she going to tell him?

Oh, hello mister security man. I don't know these people; I have never been here. And I'm coming to meet a dominatrix who is working at their house. Oh, and don't tell anyone I was here.

She scoffed and pulled up to the window.

An older, plump Hispanic man slid the glass window back and smiled genially, "Good evening, Ma'am. Where are you headed?"

Jan did her best to return the friendly smile, "Honestly, I have no idea where I'm going. It's my first time visiting, so could you tell me which way to head?" she read him the address.

"Ah, yes. Mister Abrams said to expect you. Pull straight ahead, take your first left and it will be on your left. Look for the big white house with the red brick patio and white columns. They have a pull through driveway with lighting along it to the house. You can't miss it."

"Thank you."

"Enjoy your night, miss." He smiled and with a press of a button the heavy iron gate slid silently aside.

As she pulled through the entrance of the gated community, she realized that this wasn't an average neighborhood. This was a collection of homes, each worth a couple million or more.

Jan parked in the driveway, just in front of the double doors. And, as if on cue the front door opened.

The same tall Amazon beauty from the club walked out. Brie wasn't dressed in leather but was instead in a smartly tailored skirt suit. Black with thin white pin stripping. Her skirt met just the top of her knee, and the cut of the coat was meant to accentuate every asset she had without revealing even the smallest amount of extra skin. She would look perfectly at home in any high-rise board room.

Brie walked out of the door, smiling broadly. She took Jan's hands in hers and gave her a kiss on the cheek, then leaned in and spoke softly into her ear, "I'm glad you're here, come inside." She led her by a hand.

Jan followed Brie, who seemed totally at home. She followed her through an expensively decorated and perfectly maintained entryway, that opened into a great room, which connected to an impressive kitchen. The great room had a large stone and wood fireplace, with a tame gas fire purring inside its wrought iron grate.

They continued through into the kitchen. It was, again, designed and decorated in a fashion that might grace the pages of any home and garden magazine. The floors were some sort of stone, a subtly accented golden color, with bright white grout. Travertine, Jan hazarded a guess.

The granite countertops were a similar hue of stone, with darker swirls of caramel mixed in, atop grey-blue shaker style cabinetry. The stainless appliances gleamed without a hint of a fingerprint or dust.

The room could have been a movie set, for how perfectly placed everything was, and how un-lived in it all seemed.

Brie motioned for her to sit at the wooden stools settled in a nook beneath the massive center island, "Sit."

Jan sat at the dinette bar stool. A moment later Brie handed her a drink, and said, "You have been on my mind all week. I was afraid you wouldn't call. I had the feeling that when I met you at the club, that you were new at exploring your fantasies."

"Yes. This is all new." Jan took a long pull of the red wine she had been proffered. It was an earthy red, with subtle notes of cherry. Delicious.

"It's ok. Explore as much or as little as you desire. Did you enjoy your time at encounters?"

"Yes, I did."

"Would you like to have another experience like it sometime?"

"Yes."

"Good. Finish your drink and I'll show you something."

It didn't take Jan long to finish her drink at the promise in Brie's voice. As she drained the last sip from her stemless wine glass, Brie rose and led her by the hand again. They walked through the living room, around a corner.

Brie led Jan's hand passed her, and pointed to a door, cracked just slightly, and stood aside.

"Go and see. If you're interested, try out this fantasy. If not, that's ok too." Brie smiled knowingly, "But I think you'll enjoy what you find behind the door."

Jan's heart sped up at the offer, and she walked through the door.

`*`

A Different Fantasy

Jan had, up until the night she had met Brie, had mostly a vanilla sex life. Well, that wasn't quite honest. Her partners, both men and women, preferred very vanilla sex, even if Jan herself wanted more. When alone she had watched videos of more adventurous types of sex.

So, when she crossed the threshold into the room Brie led her into she wasn't shocked. She had even seen some of the things in that room be used in some of those videos. But she had never used them herself.

The room was quite large, it could have functioned as a very respectable master bedroom for the house, but Jan assumed this wasn't their master, more so a room they kept locked. The walls were the same warm colors as the rest of the house, but the dimmer lighting made them seem deeper.

At the center of the room was a huge circular bed, it was made with a crisp white fitted sheet, and various pillows. Its headboard and frame were upholstered with plush black leather. In contrast with the soft edges of the circular bed and mattress the headboard was a rectangular back at one end of the bed. Its pleated cushions were lit with an internal glow of a light somewhere within the upper frame, aimed down to spill soft golden tones down onto the surface should the lights be fully out.

At each corner of the headboard there were purposefully placed bonds, to tie a participant by two limbs, wrists, or ankles. The high ceilings and dimensions of the room were enough to keep the huge bed from overwhelming the room.

On the far side of the room behind the bed was an oddly shaped chair. If Jan hadn't of seen one used she would have just assumed it was some foreign design. She had heard them called a tantric chair. It was shaped with two humps, one lower, one higher, to allow for different sexual positions.

To the left of the room was a tall structure shaped like an X, with well used leather ties at each end of the X. It didn't take a genius to see what that was for.

Next to that, was a something she had never seen before. This structure was shaped in an upside-down U, powder coated black, with a cross bar approximately waist height from the floor. The cross bar had a heavily padded platform, upholstered in red leather. At one side of that platform were two cuffs attached with a bright silver chain. Hanging from the top of the structure were two more cuffs, also attached by chain.

On the right of the room was a swing suspended from a black metal frame. The swing was, again, made of leather, with a plush looking red velvet pillow purpose built to fit into the main swing. Hanging along the anchor chains at each corner of the center rectangular seat were black cuffs.

Next to the swing was a wall of toys, presented in a clean organized way. The paddles, whips and cuffs were hung neatly in rows on hooks. The other toys were suspended on custom shelving that kept them secure and visible without ruining the flow of the room.

Jan looked back at Brie, "Should you decide to join us tonight, it will be you and I, and a couple. They're in their forties. In great shape, and attractive. They would like to spend the evening exploring their toys and bodies with you. I will be directing the festivities." She brushed a stray hair from Jan's check, and caressed the skin there as she did, "If not, I would like to give you a call and see you again in any fashion you'd like. Either is fine."

Jan's eyes lingered on Brie's. Brie was a tall woman, just over six feet. She was strong physically and strong in presence. Her body was supremely feminine. A small waist, wide hips, and a lush bosom. Her skin was milky white, her hair the color of honey, pulled back into a high, tight bun. She was put together with such care and attention that she should have been a photoshopped cover girl. Yet here she was. Her blue eyes waiting for Jan's decision. Jan knew that Brie was honest, she would honor whatever decision Jan made, but in that instant, the idea of following Brie's every whim was more intoxicating than the wine she had just finished.

"I'd like to stay."

"Excellent." Brie's lips curled into a smile, "Go ahead and undress. Put the towel on the bed around you and make yourself comfortable. I will be back in a moment with Mister and Missus."

`*`

Jan stripped out of her clothes and wrapped the towel around her. She settled onto the bed side and waited for the door to open. She didn't have to wait long.

The door opened; Brie entered first, carrying a stemless glass of wine. She held the door open for the couple. The man was Brie's height and muscled. He was dressed simply, in a black t-shirt and blue shorts. He had light brown hair, brushed back, in the dim light Jan couldn't tell what color his eyes were but they were a light color. He was handsome, but not overly so.

The woman was smaller, and petite. She was a couple inches shorter than Jan, approximately five foot six. Her dark hair was cut into a short bob, and she was dressed in a short black slip, made of glossy silk. She locked eyes with Jan instantly, and held her gaze, smiling softly.

Brie closed the door behind them, "Darling, I'd like you to meet Jack and Jill. I'd like you both to meet Darling. She'll be spending the next few hours with us." Brie walked over to the tantric chair and settled back into it, propping the pillow behind her so she could view the room.

"Nice to meet you both."

"You as well." Jill said still smiling.

"Jill why don't you go undress Darling." Brie directed.

The woman, Jill, walked across the room and came to stand in front of Jan. She offered Jan her hand, and Jan took it. When she was to her feet, Jan was slightly taller than Jill as she had guessed and looked down to the very petite woman.

"Hi." She said. Her nerves kept her voice quiet as she looked over the woman before her.

"Hi." Jill said sweetly, "May I?"

Jan nodded.

Jill's delicate hands reached up and untucked the knot just above her breasts. The plush towel fell in one fluid motion to the floor.

Jan locked eyes with the woman in front of her, but heard Brie say, "Good, now Jack."

Jill broke eye contact first. She turned obediently and stood in front of her husband. She pulled his shirt over his head, standing on her tippy toes to do so, then her hands started to unbuckle his shorts.

He was already hard with anticipation, the soft fabric of his shorts tented from his erection. Jan looked from the couple to Brie, and the woman was watching silently, sipping on the deep red wine in her glass.

Jill let the shorts fall and her husband stepped out of the shorts, his cock bounced in anticipation in time with the beat of his heart.

"Get on your knees." Brie directed, "Darling, go pick a toy from the wall and make yourself comfortable on the bed. Enjoy the show."

Jan obediently walked over to the wall and chose a pink vibrator, approximately twelve inches in length and a couple inches in girth. She laid back on the bed, tucking pillows behind her so that she was propped up to watch as Jill took Jack into her mouth.

Jan twisted the end of the vibrator to turn it on, and it buzzed to life, quiet for how ferociously it shook. She brought it to her center, relishing the sensation.

Jill took her husband into her mouth without hesitation. She brought her hand up to work his thickness, moving it in time with the motions of her mouth.

Jack brought his hands to her head, brushing her hair back and cradling it in his fingers, keeping it away from her face. As he did, he reflexively thrust his hips forward slightly causing Jill to gag softly.

Jan watched them together. Moving with familiarity. Her body responded to the show and the vibrations, slickening with anticipation for what was to come. She could feel the pressure build within herself. Her gaze slipped over to Brie, who was looking at Jan instead of the couple. Her eyes watching her every move hungrily.

The look in Brie's eyes was enough to send Jan over into her first orgasm of the night. Her hips rocked with the ebb and flow of it, and she moaned along with the motion, softly at first then more urgently as the climax continued to ride its waves.

Brie smiled over her wine as she took another sip, "Good, enough. Jack I want you to take Darling."

Jill pulled away from her husband, wiping her lips, she was flushed and breathing heavily.

Jack obeyed Brie's wishes. He walked over and tentatively reached towards Jan.

"Darling, I never said you could stop with that toy. He'll just have to work around it." Brie said.

Jan smiled brightly. She repositioned the vibrator so that it wasn't directly contacting her swollen, sensitive clit. It was so soon after her first orgasm that she couldn't bare it directly. So, she teased herself. Her body prickled when Jack touched her, timidly caressing the flesh of her calf at first. His hand was lightly calloused, only enough to add a delicious texture to his feather soft touch as his fingers danced across the skin there.

Jan moaned softly at his touch, and his cock twitched in response to her sounds. He took that as approval and brought his hand to her other foot. His hands first touched her around her ankles, each hand brushing gently in time with the other up towards her legs. At the bend of her knees his hands hooked beneath the knees and pulled her closer to the edge of the bed.

Jan dropped her knees wider.

His eyes devoured the view, never lingering on one spot, but rather trying to take a mental image of all of her.

Jack climbed on the bed with her. The weight of him made the mattress dip slightly as he rested onto his knees and looked her over again. Jan returned the favor. He was so perfectly muscled, not too heavily, but in a way that made him look supremely masculine. His chest was sparsely peppered with dark hair that trailed seductively down toward his manhood. Her eyes had followed that trail and eyed him hungrily. He wasn't enormous but he was impressive. And thick.

He was painfully hard at the thought of fucking her in front of the other women. And Jan agreed. Her womanhood slickened and clenched with need.

Her eyes flitted up to his face, as his strong hands (they were so big!) cradled her right calf first; seductively playing with her skin there. When he reached her knees his right hand slipped away and began stroking his cock, while his left drug his nails across her skin.

Each caress of his hands made her body react with shocking intensity. That little voice that told her what was appropriate and what she *should* do was gone, replaced with a demanding voice, telling her *Yes! This is what you need! This is everything you wanted and then some!*

Her heart raced so fast she was sure Jill should be able to see it beating against her ribs, but she couldn't take her eyes from Jack's hand as it stroked his manhood.

"You won't fuck her until I say you can." Brie said simply.

He took his time, letting those strong hands explore each inch of her legs as he moved himself upward. Her legs instinctively opened to allow him to climb further between.

He relinquished his cock, and ran his lusciously rough hands up her hips, then he climbed further, his hips meeting hers. She could feel him then, how hard and ready he was. He was painfully swollen. The hardness of his cock demanded satisfaction, demanded that she give him that.

But still he waited.

"Lay your cock on her, I want to see how deep you'll go." Brie sat up straighter to get a better view.

Jack did as he was told. He placed himself against the neatly hair wreathing her womanhood.

"You can play with her all you want but you won't fuck her until I say so." Brie reminded him.

"Yes, ma'am." Jack agreed. His eyes ran over her, as if he were trying to gather his thoughts to figure something else to do. Then he drug the nails of his fingers up her hips to her sides and then to her breasts. He didn't squeeze her as many men did when given the chance, but instead cupped each breast gently in a hand. Then he leaned forward and brought his lips down between her breasts, then trailed his warm kisses down to her stomach. She squirmed beneath him, and at her movements a sound of pure desire escaped his lips, rumbling against her sensitive skin.

When he reached the pouch of her stomach he worked his way back up and as he did, his mouth claimed her right breast; the searing heat of his lips tore a gasp, then a moan from her.

He played his tongue around the suddenly hard nipple in his mouth. The sensation of him sucking, gently nibbling, and teething at her made her writhe in his arms.

"Fuck her."

He released his hold on her breast and in an instant he was back on his knees.

Jan watched as he again stroked himself between her legs, he was fully erect in front of her, as if letting her size, him up, and oh she did just that.

The look in his eyes was suddenly animalistic. He was going to devour her, one way or another and she wanted him to, so badly.

He braced his weight with his left hand as his right came down to angle him between her legs, and he pressed the head of his cock against the slickness of her opening.

"Ah, ah! Jill why don't you put your husband into Darling?"

Jill obediently crossed the room and grabbed her husband's cock, she positioned him perfectly for entry and his hips instinctively jerked forward, and in an instant he filled her.

Jan could do nothing but gasp.

Then Jill took the vibrator from Jan's hand and climbed onto the bed next to her. She placed it perfectly onto Jan's swollen clit, no mercy for how sensitive she still was, and in the moment that it took Jack to find a rhythm Jan came again.

Her moans melded with the grunts of Jack as he fully sheathed himself into her again and again. His thrusts were urgent but not aggressive.

He was so wide she could feel him stretch her walls, where they wrapped tightly around him, to accommodate him. Her body demanded more, wanted all of him, immediately.

Just as the tremors of her climax allowed her to form some semblance of thought, he withdrew a moment, brought her leg over her body, and held both together above his shoulder. He smiled as he slid into her. She moaned in time with his hips, as her body was suddenly wracked with a second, stronger orgasm and he kept a slow pace, relishing the feel of her wrapping his cock in her.

Without thinking about it she reached over and began to return the favor to Jill. She was at an odd angle to finger her clit with her index finger, but she could work her thumb just as well. Jill was so wet it was hard to get enough friction on her, but Jan managed.

Her legs shook so badly that she was sure she would spasm and knock Jack from his perch on the end of the bed.

And just then, as Jill began to work her hips against Jan's hand, Jill brought her right hand came down teased Jan's nipple, rolling the sensitive bud between her thumb and forefinger.

His thrust became deeper, longer. In her ecstasy sensitive pussy, she could feel every vein of his cock, every velvety fold of him.

"You can come, Jack." Brie said softly.

Jill leaned away from Jan, and Jack grunted at the order. His masculine hands shifted her. Somehow, without pulling fully out of her, he positioned her on her stomach, and one of his strong hands came down on her back, holding her down beneath him.

Jan had womanly hips, and a big ass, so in this position he couldn't fully push into her, but she got enough of him to feel his cock swell as if it would burst. His strokes felt as if they might cleave her in half, and since she couldn't see him in this position, her eyes finally found Brie.

Sometime during their performance, Brie had finished her drink and donned her strap on. Not only that, she had Jill on her knees and was taking her from behind, positioned perfectly to watch Jack fuck Jan.

Brie eyed her hungrily. Her pussy tightened around him at the thought. She wanted her. Brie wanted to be inside her, wanted to be in Jack's position.

She could just hear over the thundering of her heart, directions from Brie.

"Fill her up."

"Cum on her tits!"

"Fuck her harder!"

"Make her scream!"

Words that echoed her own thoughts, and if she could speak over her own moans she would tell him to listen. Do what she said dammit!

He thrust into her harder, bottoming out in her cunt. Her body bucked at the fullness, but even that pain somehow turned to hot pleasure within her. The feel of him reaching her end nearly made her cum again.

The weight of him pressing her down was so dominating it was almost as much a turn on as when he had been between her legs.

He growled with need and his motion became faster, deeper, taking her fully. His cock claimed her from within; his hand pinning her down released its hold. And both came down around her hips. And he did as she pleased.

He fucked her harder. Faster still.

The sounds of her own pleasure as she came a mind shattering third time deafened her. Her hips had a mind of their own, coming up to meet each of his thrusts, in primal need.

His fingers dug into her hips, and his thrusts became more urgent. As she felt his body clench with the promise of an explosive orgasm of his own, in the last moment, her pulled away from inside her. The length of his impressive sex was nothing compared to how hard he came. His climax spurted load after load of hot, sweet cum onto her ass. his own voice now lost to the moans of his orgasm.

She arched her hips to him, taking each spray of him onto her, enjoying the feel of this ancient form of claim.

"Very good. Take a break, Jack."

Her Turn

On her back again, catching her breath. Jan had expected that Brie would fuck her next, she instead led Jill over to her and down to her knees. Shen her head dropped between her thighs Jan inhaled sharply.

Jill's tongue curled first into her, exploring her depths, as she moaned at the feeling of her. Then she found Jan's center. Her hips bucked as her lips sucked on Jan's clit, then released her and circled around it, flicking, and teasing her, before again penetrating her, she moaned into her, lapping at the juices she wrought from her. Her hand came up to join her mouth. The pressure and rhythm she found had Jan gasping for air. Her hands instinctively wrapped into Jill's hair.

The pressure from Jill's hands brought her dangerously close to orgasm, but she slowed just as her breathing became ragged. That searing tongue was all she could focus on, and then she was suddenly abandoned.

Jill rose from where she claimed her and stepped back.

Brie mounted the bed next.

There was a time that the idea of giving over total control to someone would have been terrifying. Now it wasn't as terrifying as it was freeing.

Total release.

Jan had a feeling Brie wouldn't let her down.

Brie wasted no time. She squared her weight between Jan's legs, "Jill, get yourself a toy and come touch Darling for me while I fuck her." Brie then brought the pink vibrator Jan had been using directly to Jan's clit as she began to finger her. Turned to its highest setting, the sudden sensation made her hips buck involuntarily. In response, Brie delved three fingers deep into her, "Ah, ah! Don't move."

She began to fuck her with those fingers as she teased Jan closer and closer to another climax. Jan's body shivered at the urgency, the need to move her hips in time with the motion of the woman ruling her. Brie ignored her and added a fourth finger, fucking her with her entire hand, as the vibrator wrenched the slickness from her, giving Brie the lubrication she needed.

She quickened the pace of her hand, back and forth, testing her walls, putting more force behind it. The pain and pleasure mixed together until Jan was sure she could take no more.

Then, satisfied, Brie withdrew her hand, now coated in the evidence of Jan's arousal, and positioned her hips between Jan's legs.

Sometime during, Jill had done as she was told and gotten a vibrator. She lay next to Jan, dragging the back of her perfectly manicured nails along the delicate flesh of Jan's breast nearest her.

Brie brought down her left hand, rubbed whatever juices she still had on that hand along the artificial shaft, and pressed the head of the massive cock against her pussy. It was too big, no way it would fit, Jan writhed beneath her, as Brie pressed her hips harder forward.

Even though she was very ready for it, Jan still cried out as the strap on slid home, finally pressing pass the tightness of her pussy. It slid in with suck force, her first thrust put Brie's fake cock halfway into her. And halfway of a fantastical amount of girth and length that would never be found on a man was nearly too much already.

Brie brought both hands down onto Jan's shoulders, holding her still as she began to thrust, slowly increasing her rhythm. The woman was so much stronger than Jan it wasn't even a fight. Besides she wanted this oh so badly.

"Jack, fuck your wife. Hard." Brie said between thrusts. Jan looked over and sure enough he was already hard again.

Jan moaned and cried out, as each thrust filled her deeper, fuller. Brie grunted as well, each time she slapped her hips forward. She grabbed the still buzzing vibrator with her left hand and pressed it harshly against Jan's abused clit. Bringing her passed the brink again. As Jan moaned along with the spasms of her body Brie grunted and sped up her thrust, "That's it, come for me baby."

Brie's left hand slid over to the crest of Jan's neck and she pressed with the expertise that came from practice. She knew just how to choke her. Press in just the right way that that heady feeling overtook Jan, but she could still breath. Spots danced across her vision, and though she heard her own screams, she wasn't sure if she came again, or if Brie had just drawn out the last orgasm.

Brie moved her hand back to Jan's shoulders and moved the vibrator beneath Jan. Bringing the rapidly moving shaft to her back entrance. She pressed the pointed pink end against the pucker of Jan's ass. Jan was so wet, and Brie had been fucking her so roughly that her slickness had made its way there too.

She moaned louder, as Brie teased her ass, "You're going to get it there another night. Don't worry."

She timed her thrusts, alternating between the vibrator penetrating Jan, and the massive cock, until Jan couldn't count the number of orgasms she had been forced into. In truth she wasn't sure she had ever stopped coming.

Jan wasn't sure if it had taken hours or minutes, but sometime after, she realized that Brie had pulled out of her, and was wiggling out of her straps, "Stay right there. You're going to get me off next."

Jan said nothing. She focused on her breathing, trying to catch her breath. She hardly noticed Brie had climbed up onto the bed again and was positioning her hips above Jan's waiting mouth. Without a word, she lowered her blonde curls down onto Jan's face.

Jan's own carnal instinct took over. The sweet tanginess of Brie's pussy made her mouth water. She brought her hand up, but Brie batted it away, and brought the vibrator to her own clit, so Jan focused on her tongue.

"Jack, come on my tits." She said simply with a purr. Jan had forgotten all about the couple. Jill lay there spent, watching the women next to her, as her husband pulled out of her and got to his feet on the bed. He pleasured himself watching Jan work Brie's pussy.

Brie tongued at her juices and rocked her head to get into a better position. Brie brought her other hand down and pulled at Jan's hair, "That's it, right there." So, Jan repeated herself, fucking the blonde with her tongue until she felt Brie's body clench with her own orgasm.

As Brie moaned softly, Jack grunted loudly, and spurted himself all over Brie's impressive its. As soon as Brie was finished, she dismounted. She collected her things and returned them to her purse, then set it on the chair in Jan's corner, "Why don't you use the shower in this room Darling? I'll take the one in the hall."

Monday

Jan smiled at the text on her phone. It was from Brie.

It was just another Monday, but she had had another weekend like no other. Brie had followed her home after they had cleaned up at Jack and Jill's. They had talked all night and spent the next morning and afternoon together.

Brie was very witty, no surprise to Jan. What had been a surprise was how quickly the weekend had passed and how much she looked forward to the next time she saw the dominatrix.

She hadn't expected their first meeting, or their second. She hadn't expected she would have ever had the courage to call the white embossed numbers on that gloss black business card of Brie's.

She wasn't sure what to expect from their relationship, or if they would even have one besides drinks and lunch and the occasional night of fantasy, but she had decided that she wasn't going to put pressure on it. Whatever came of their time together, she would have memories that no one else could give her.

Besides it was nice to look forward to a text again.

If you enjoyed this story, please leave a Review or Rating to let us know!

Follow Autumn Greer on Amazon for notifications of new stories, and visit us at AutumnGreer.com to subscribe to our newsletter!

An Excerpt From:

Sleeping with the Enemy

Sasha was on all fours, the roundness of her ass held high, and her shoulders held firmly by the naked woman behind her. She was breathless. The last few days she had spent a lot of time just like that, unable to catch her breath and keep up with her insatiable counterpart.

She took a deep breath and could smell the subtle jasmine perfume of the woman above her, the clean sheets beneath her body had been changed by the maids. What must they think of the sounds coming from her bedroom? Hell, Sasha had never heard herself make sounds like that before either. Her cleaning ladies were quick, and discreet, and had made a quick exit before the pair had returned to the room.

The lithe and commanding woman who held her with such dominance was wearing a strap on, and sliding it slowly inside Sasha.

“I knew I was going to like fucking you." Annette’s sultry voice purred above her. She had the voice of a phone sex operator, smoky and full of promise of soon to be had pleasure.

Sasha felt helpless. Deliciously so.

She had already been subjected to having her shoulders pinned while lying on her back by the woman's knees as she lowered herself onto Sasha's waiting tongue. That had not completely satiated the dominate red head. After which, when Sasha had returned from pouring them both an iced white wine, and after indulging therein, Sasha had been placed in the position she now found herself.

Other Titles by Autumn Greer:

***Be sure to follow Autumn Greer on her Author Page** Here*

Titles featuring The Man:

The Club: A Game of Choice

The Man visits The Club, a swingers' club. There, he is asked to join a Game of Choice by a Porn Star. Three Husbands get to spend time with the Star. Three wives get to choose three mystery single men from The Club to spend 60 seconds with, then choose one to spend thirty minutes with. Will he be chosen?

The Club: A Married Woman's Debut

A husband goes to The Club without his Wife, so she does the same. While there she meets The Man. Will this be her first and last time at The Club? Or will she be its newest regular?

The Club: Submissive

The Man brings a friend to The Club, and she's all tied up. With three couples, three single men and The Man, what's a girl to do?

The Visitor: An Anniversary Gift

Annie's husband finds her search history by accident and arranges to have her deepest fantasy become a reality. Joel finds a Visitor who can grant these desires, in ways even Annie didn't think was possible. The visitor shows this couple what true passion can be and takes the lead to make this Anniversary Gift one to remember.

Titles featuring other Alpha Males:

Amateur Night

A college student hears of a place that the woman is in control of the night and allowed to make her wildest fantasies come true. She's never done anything like this before, but will a night with three men be the liberating experience she's been waiting for?

Behind Locked Doors

An irresistible neighbor, named Vlad, asks Sarah to water his plants while he is away. Inside, she finds a locked door. What's behind that door is more enticing than she could have ever imagined. Behind Locked Doors will show you what Vlad is hiding and leave you begging for more!

Business Affairs Book 1 & 2

Book 1:

Corinne thought she had seen the last of Paul, but on the night celebrating her biggest success he shows up, bring back memories of their first night together. An encounter she will never forget. Will this be the last she sees of him?

Book 2:

Paul offers Corinne a new experience. This one with two stunning blonde women. Will indulging in what she thought was a forbidden desire give Corinne the confidence she's been lacking?

The Drummer: Inside the Tour Bus

Victoria's two best friends drag her out to a performance by a band she's never heard of, and boy is she glad they did. When the drummer of the band only has eyes for her will Victoria take a chance that is totally out of character for her, and see where it leads?

The Neighbor Comes Calling

A jealous neighbor tries to move in on Tina's boyfriend, with Tina there, but her boyfriend has another idea all together for the night.

Changing Jobs & Changing Partners

Cherry has no choice but to fire Dylan. But as he's leaving, she realizes this might be her last chance to find out if he wants her as much as she wants him.

They're both married, and now she is his ex-boss. This can't turn out well. Or can it? Dylan invites Cherry and her husband to dinner at his house, with his wife. His very attractive, very bisexual wife. What happens when you swap partners with your ex-employee? What happens when that employee's wife wants you and your husband?

Speed Dating

A handsome stranger takes a lucky speed dater out for the experience she never knew she needed. A businessman named Tony, a mysterious club within a club, and a live performance that involves dropping all the barriers she has ever had. Stephanie learns that excitement can come from the least likely places, and along the way she might learn a little about herself and what she's been missing.

Stop and Go

She has had enough of her soon to be mother-in-law calling her a whore. If she thought she was a slut, then she would be one! A truck stop on the way how is sure to be the most exciting stop her and her fiancé have ever had!

Romantic Erotica

The Coffee Shop

After breaking up with her cheating boyfriend, on the drive home from a business trip, Nessa meets and falls for a handsome Army Ranger. Will this chance meeting be their one and only time together? Or is this the start of something to last?

The Job Interview

Ellie needs this job. She's behind on every bill she has, and she is so damned close to finishing her degree she can taste it, but when her interviewer is not only the most handsome man she has ever laid eyes on, but also the most interesting, is she having dinner with him to secure her position in the company? Or looking for something else entirely?

Time Goes Slowly

Charlotte is bored. She tired of the same old too-polite, quiet guys, the same old dates, with terribly droll conversation. And she is determined to make a change.

When she finds an ad online, describing not only what the mysterious poster wants to do to her, but what he expects her to do while he does it, she is intrigued. Will he be the change she so earnestly craves?

Western Alpha Male Erotica:

A Cowboy Affair

Jane is a successful businesswoman, in a company dominated by men. When her firm decides to rent out a western themed Dude Ranch for a team building retreat, she goes along. World class fishing, cowboys, horses, and beautiful Colorado, who could resist? Jane is faced with two choices. Spend time with her colleague's wives or go on a trail ride with one of the most attractive men she's ever laid eyes on. What's a city girl to do?

Titles Featuring Alpha Females:

Sleeping with the Enemy

Sasha has something Bart wants, and Bart has something Sasha wants. Bart agrees on one condition: Sasha must spend two nights with his Dominant wife, Annette. Sasha has always wanted Annette, but will she be able to give herself over fully to the other woman's will?

Encounters

For a week Jan had been having the same dream. She was tied and blindfolded. A dominant woman's voice controlling the men's every action. Over a two-mimosa brunch she shared the dream with an old friend from college. Her Friend knows a place that will make her dream a reality.

Collections:

*The Fantasy Collection**: Forbidden Desires Brought to Life Steamy Erotica Short Stories*** (Amateur Night; The Club: Submissive; & Behind Locked Doors)

Suddenly Taken Collection: ***Erotica Stories to Spend the Night With*** (Changing Jobs & Changing Partners; Speed Dating; Stop and Go)

The Stranger: ***A Collection of Intense Erotica*** (The Visitor; The Club: A Game of Choice; The Club: Debut; A Neighbor Comes Calling)

Sweetly His: ***A Collection of Romantic Erotica Short Stories*** (The Coffee Shop; The Job Interview; Time Goes Slowly; and a sneak peek at Business Affairs 1)

www.ingramcontent.com/pod-product-compliance
Lightning Source LLC
LaVergne TN
LVHW040925150826
845672LV00007B/2204

* 9 7 9 8 7 5 0 9 2 8 0 3 3 *